Why?

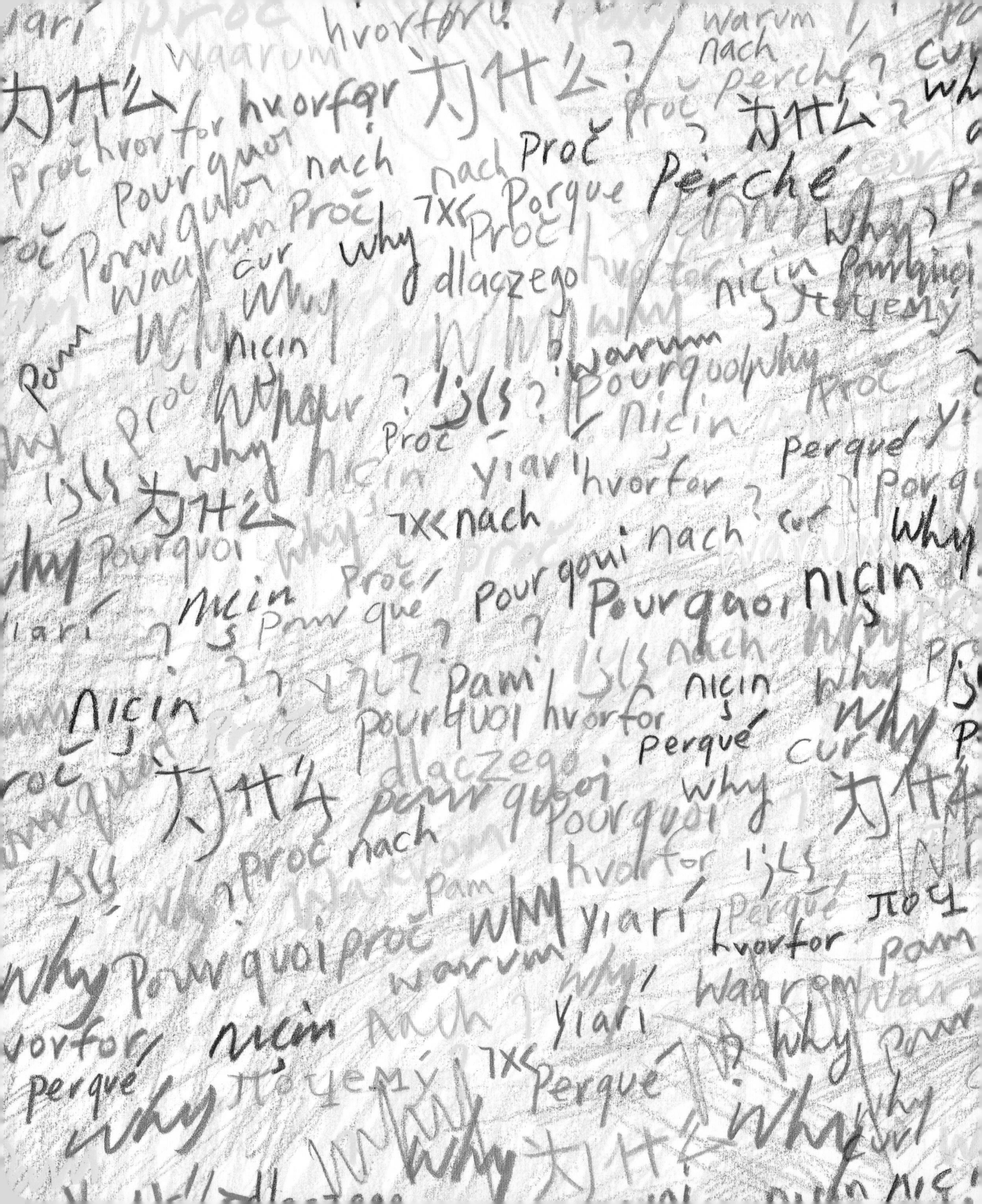

hvorfor
warum
nach
为什么
perché
hvorfor
Proč
pourquoi
nach
Porque
Perché
waarom
why
dlaczego
niçin
cur
warum
pourquoi
why
Proč
perque
yiari
hvorfor
nach
cur
pourquoi
nach
pourqoui
Pourquoi
niçin
Pour que
pam
niçin
pourquoi
hvorfor
perqué
cur
why
dlaczego
pourquoi
nach
hvorfor
pam
yiari
hvorfor
pourquoi
proč
warum
waarom
yiari
niçin
perque
Perque
why

dlaczego warum ?j(? 7x< ?j(? γιζ hvor
7x< why? Perqué yiari ? niçin pam Porque
nach hvorfor Proč Pourqoi Pourquoi? why why ? Proč why
?j(? 7x< cur niçin hvorfor hvorfor why why
γιζ pam niçin hvorfor pourquoi? warum ?j(? Perch
yiari niçin pourquoi warum ?)++< why why Joyem
Proč γιζ waarom Proč pourquoi our quoi why why
why why? why perque why pourquoi why
dlaczego? yiari why pourquoi why 7x<
why pourquoi? nach why proč
wquoi ?j(? ? nach waarom why why
proč cur pourquoi γιζ nach pam why why
? j(? yiari dlaczego niçin proč why
yiari waarom Proč ? perque
dlaczego proč yiari proč Pour quoi Perché pro
quoi 7x< yiari proč γιζ niçin nach why W
yiari niçin proč? dlaczego 7x< nac
niçin? Pourquoi. dlaczego 7x< pam
?)++< why ?j(? why proč)++

For Laura. Why? It just is - L.C.
For Abigail and Penguin - T.R.

Published by Hinkler Books Pty Ltd
45–55 Fairchild Street
Heatherton Victoria 3202 Australia
www.hinklerbooks.com

hinkler

First published by Andersen Press Ltd., London

Text © Lindsay Camp 1998
Illustrations © Tony Ross 1998
Cover design © Hinkler Books 2010

Cover design: Peter Tovey
Prepress: Graphic Print Group

ISBN: 978 1 7418 4433 7

Printed and bound in China

Why?

written by Lindsay Camp
illustrated by Tony Ross

There was one thing Lily did that drove her dad mad.

Actually, it wasn't a thing she *did*.

It was a thing she said.

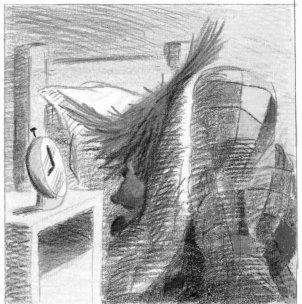

She said it all the time.

She said it first thing in the morning.

It's time you were dressed.

Why?

She said it at breakfast time.

She said it when they went shopping.

She said it when her dad read her a story.

And of course, she said it at bedtime.

Usually, Lily's dad

did his best to explain.

Because it rained all last night.

Why?

Because there were lots of big black clouds full of tiny drops of water.

Why?

Because . . . well, there just were, Lily.

There just were!

But sometimes, when he was a bit tired or too busy,

he'd just get cross.

Then, one Friday, something rather unusual happened.

Lily was playing in the sandpit in the park.

Suddenly, Lily's dad stopped and looked upwards. So did Lily.
And so did everybody else in the park.

Lily was too astonished to say anything. After all, she'd never seen a gigantic Thargon spaceship before.

The Thargon spaceship came lower, and then it landed in the park, right next to the sandpit.

Everybody stood and stared. The doors of the spaceship slid open

and out squelched several Thargons.

They didn't look very friendly.

The most important Thargon oozed forward.

Everyone started to tremble.

Everyone except Lily, that is.

The chief Thargon turned to his friends. He looked thoughtful.

Lily and her dad and all the other people watched as they talked together in Thargish for quite a long time.

Then the chief Thargon slithered forward again, and spoke to Lily.

Lily was just about to say something

but her dad put his hand over her mouth,

just in time.

That night at bedtime, when he'd finished reading her a story,

Lily's dad gave her an extra big hug.

And then he promised he'd never get cross with her again,
no matter how often she asked him why.

I was very proud
of you in the park
today.

Why?

为什么 Proč hvorfor? warum nach Perché? cur why
Pourquoi nach Porque Perché
Proč cur why 为什么 dlaczego niçin Pourquoi Proč
niçin warum Pourquoi why Proč
为什么 why niçin yiari hvorfor perqué Pourquo
Pourquoi nach niçin Proč nach cur why
niçin Proč Pour que Pourquoi Pourquoi niçin
为什么 dlaczego perqué cur why 为什么
nach Pourquoi hvorfor why 为什么
Proč nach Pam yiari perqué почму pam
why Pourquoi Proč why yiari hvorfor why pam
hvorfor niçin nach yiari why pam
perqué почму Perqué why 为什么 why